For Arie, whose love for her animals is pure and inspiring.
I love you, my baby girl.

If you
give a
girl a
chicken

you
better
give her
two.

Three or four
is better!

That's what she will say to you.

The girl
will be
so
happy

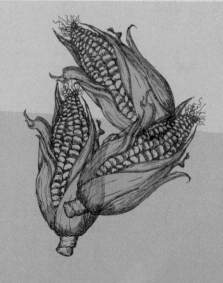

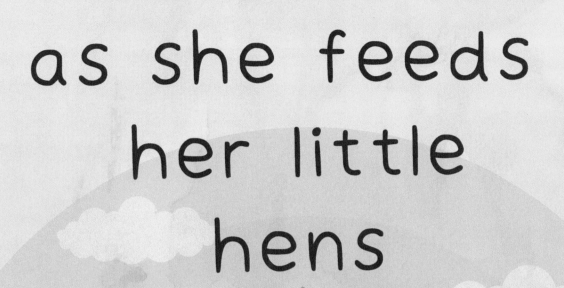

as she feeds her little hens

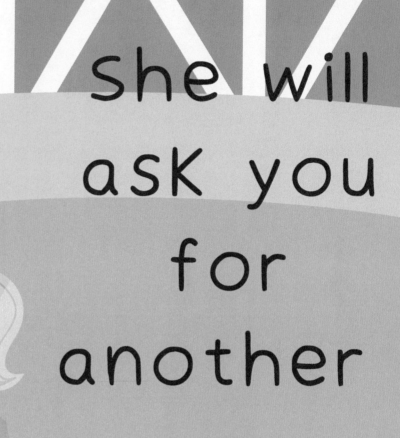

she will
ask you
for
another

and
then
she'll
ask
again.

The girl will love those chickens,

she will make it
clearly known.

She will love
them when
they're little,

and even more when they are grown.

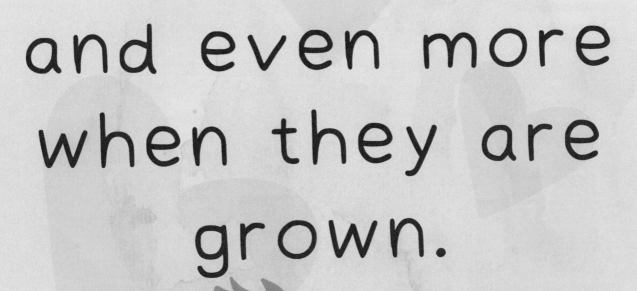

she will take
the time to
hold them

and handle them with care.

She will let
them climb up
on her head,

her arms -

everywhere!

she will check on them in evening

before it's time for bed.

She will go to sleep with visions

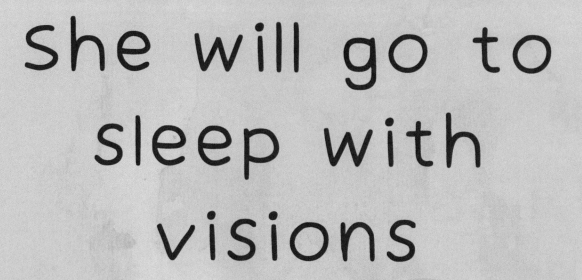

of those
chickens
in her
head.

A dog is great and dandy.

A cat
is
okay,
too.

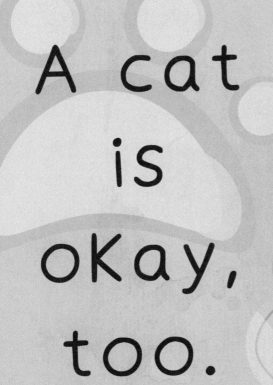

But, if you give a girl a chicken

you better give
her two!

Made in the USA
Middletown, DE
05 April 2023